WOMAN

Monologues for Actresses
(Ten One-Act Scenes)

Susan Pomerance

Dramaline Publications

Dramaline Publications
36-851 Palm View Road
Rancho Mirage, CA 92270
Phone 619/770-6076 Fax 619/770-4507

Cover art by John Sabel

This book is printed on 55# Glatfelter acid-free paper, a paper that meets the requirements of the American Standard of Permanence of paper for printed library material.

CONTENTS

A word about *Woman*: Each monologue has been purposefully written of an extended duration in the interest of flexibility. They may, if desired, be cut to fit the needs of individual situations, presented as is as one-act scenes, or presented as an evening of theatre by several actresses or a single actress as a one-woman show.

Darlene, A Shirt-Sleeve Self-Starter

DARLENE

Darlene tells of her job-hunting travails. We find her working diligently at her typewriter. She stops typing, and turns toward us in a reflective attitude which she maintains for a few seconds before relaxing and speaking to us with an air of casual honesty.

I looked. I schlepped. And without a car, it was no picnic, let me tell you. Riding crowded buses from morning till night, going from interview to interview, rubbing elbows with sweaty people who obviously weren't comfortable with deodorant . . . it was damned hard to stay perky. By the end of the day, I was pretty well perked out. After working for Howards & Crumwell for almost ten years, it was a bitch coming to grips with job hunting. But I had to make the move, get out, make a change. They all said I was crazy for just up and leaving like that without something else, you know. But the thought of one more boring, endless day at H & C, doing the same boring job at the same desk, drinking too much of the same old, weak, flavorless coffee . . . it was just too much. So I quit. They all tried to talk me into staying, told me how invaluable I was, how I was part of "the family." They even offered me more money. That was tempting, I have to admit. But after thinking it over, I knew it wasn't a question of money; it was a matter of doing something new with my life, with breaking the mold, with busting loose. I just had to pick myself up and move myself, make a drastic, radical move. It was inside me, pushing out, this thing, this feeling compelling me to get off my butt and take charge of my life—get out of the rut, you know.

So, I give two weeks' notice and they give me this big farewell party. All the big bosses came down from Hartford, even, and they gave me all kinds of neat gifts and made speeches and we all cried. Everybody was super nice. Interesting, though—I didn't hear from *any* of these people after that. That's the first thing I learned: when you're gone, you're gone—it's over. Don't hold your breath for all those people you worked with for years, and went to lunch with every day, and shared intimate feelings with, to give you a concerned follow-up call. It just doesn't happen. You change jobs—those relationships are terminal.

I took a couple of weeks off and took a trip back home and kicked back and hung out with old friends and did some shopping and the like. When I got back, I placed myself with this employment agency and they started sending me out like crazy. They said placing me would be a cinch because I was super-qualified and sharp and made a good impression.

Well, the first interview was with the president of a carpet company over on the east side. A little grease-ball with three hairs slicked over his bald head and dirty fingernails. He kept staring at my legs and making these incredibly gross sucking noises through his teeth. A miniature Hoover sweeper, this creep. Sickening. He asked me out to dinner, and of course you know what that means—it means you wind up the being the entre´e. Then there was this real dignified-looking man who was all dressed up like a store mannequin who kept checking out his reflection in a window while he asked a bunch of stupid questions. It was like he was interviewing himself, or something. I found him to be very deep on looks and very shallow on character.

Then they kept coming in rapid succession: the owner of a car dealership who, I had the feeling, wanted to test drive me in a local motel; a self-made clothing manufacturer who drove a new Rolls and wanted to pay me peanuts; a fast-food mogul who got pissed off when I told him I hated frozen peas. What a bunch of strangies. And the women were even worse. Let me tell you, because you're a woman doesn't mean a damn. I found that a lot of these professional dames take on a man's demeanor. They dress masculinely, talk with forced lowered voices, use language you wouldn't believe, and expect the moon. They just aren't looking for over-achievers, they wanna hire God. Except maybe God would be under-qualified. One of these women—Jane something or other—who was the director of one of the biggest advertising agencies in town, was truly unbelievable. She wanted to know if I was a "shirt-sleeve self-starter." Frankly, I didn't know what the hell she was talking about. In the first place, I don't wear shirts, I wear blouses. Then she asked if I had "hands-on experience interfacing with the window of corporate networking." She was something else. I kept waiting for her to whip out a cigar and strike a match with her thumbnail.

Dear, it was a nightmare, let me tell you. Thank heavens Howards & Crumwell took me back. With a nice, healthy raise, of course. And, oh yes . . . they even sprung for a new coffee maker.

I was the first star to ever come out of the water looking wet. Nobody knew what I looked like because I never looked the same way twice.

Bette Davis (1908-1989)

Kathy, Brother

KATHY

Kathy is seated on an institutional-type chair mid-stage. A single light illuminates her, isolating her up there with an ethereal glow. She is deeply predisposed, locked in heavy thought. When she speaks, she does so lugubriously, finding the subject matter hurtful.

Charles. We hadn't been intimate since we were kids. I guess that's the way it often is with brothers and sisters. They're so close that nothing's exchanged but trivialities. Of course, he was five years older than I was, and that makes a big difference between children, separates them by light years it seems. He always seemed so much older. I viewed him as an adult from the time I can remember. And I'm sure to him I was just a little, noisy, bothersome brat with juvenile fancies. We just didn't relate at all. Not that many people do, really. Most of us have this impenetrable veneer of self-protection around us that guards us from giving and absorbing emotions. I don't think Charles and I had ever said we loved each other. Not that I can remember, anyway. We grew up under the same roof, going our own ways, not connecting, each involved in our superficial life-games. There we were, like two islands—drifting. A damned shame.

When Charles went off to college, I only saw him on breaks and once in a while during summer vacation. And then, when I went off to school upstate, we just sort of became these related strangers who hugged perfunctorily at family functions and made small talk where neither listened. Frankly, I wasn't interested in his life and his writing and his arcane poetry, which turned me off completely. He always seemed such a self-righteous intellectual to me. And then, of course, there were his friends. Even as far back as high school, I thought them outrageous. There was this, this peculiarity about them, I thought, something . . . I couldn't put my finger on it. The realization didn't hit me till I was in my late teens. I guess it's difficult to recognize homosexuality in a brother or sister. Because, perhaps, you subconsciously suppress the reality of it because it carries, like, this preconceived stigma. You know—immorality, sin . . . all the other ingrained uglies. It's all so muddled and crazy and so full of prehistoric, addled thinking.

At first, I was very upset. Charles, my own brother, after all. He was an embarrassment, a horrible stain on the family and me—especially me. How could he? I didn't want anything to do with him; him and his mincy friends who, to me, were these caricatures of femininity. So, I rejected him totally, put him out of my life. I didn't approve of him or his lifestyle, and I resented the hell out of him for making my life uncomfortable. My, what a self-centered, immature, prejudiced little twerp I was.

As time passed, my attitude toward him softened considerably. Even though we never became really close, we developed this relationship. Comfortable, I guess you might say. Isn't that sickening what I just said?*Comfortable*! I realize now how destructively safe that is, how insidiously corrupting to the moral fiber. God, to hate totally or love totally without fear— how much better than some state of sequestered feelings. What a fool I was, what a damned fool!

When I learned he had AIDS, I was devastated. Suddenly a lifetime of props were kicked out from under my middle-class thinking and, for the very first time, I was faced with something. Till then, it'd been a sidelong glance at this wonderful, fragile thing called life. But now, pow!, there it was—something horrible and real and important. I was going to lose someone dear, someone dear whose feelings I'd never let get past my insensitivity. Hell, my brother. My *brother*! The word "brother," it now took on such significance. Brother, sister, me, him—*us*!

When I found out, I drove up to Boston without hesitation. Already the ravages of the disease were telling on him. He'd gotten thinner and his eyes were full of his desperation. Then everything was stripped away. And all those feelings, all those years of pent-up, held-back, buried brotherly and sisterly emotions were broken open, just like when you slice a melon and it falls apart and there you have it, the insides, the guts of it. It's amazing how honesty heals. (*Pause.*) The months that followed were difficult. Difficult for me, that is. But Charles, he faced his fate courageously, with humor and goodwill, thinking of others, preparing his friends, me, the family for the time, for . . . the end.

Charles passed away a few moments ago. It was a quiet end. I'll never forget the brightness in his eyes. It was as if his soul were suddenly neon. Mother and Father are still in there—in his room. I just had to get out, come out here in the hall for a while and be alone with my thoughts. (*She takes a paper from her purse, unfolds it.*) While I was going through his things, I came across one of his poems. (*She reads.*)

Understanding forms a dotted line that,
Thin and abstract with wavering intensity,
Circles the wilderness and
Serpentines with pulsing light along dark streets
Where fear hides in little houses.

The wavering of it can be seen only
By the few who embrace it and find wisdom,
For the others, it's merely a meaningless tendril
Wavering there beyond reach and recognition
Crying plaintively—
I'm yours
I'm yours
I'm yours.

> *To put it bluntly, I seem to be a whole superstructure with no foundation. But I'm working on the foundation.*

Marilyn Monroe (Norma Jean Baker or Mortenson, 1926-1962)

Leslie, The Blue Banlon Dream

LESLIE

Leslie enters carrying a photo album, goes to a chair mid-stage, sits, opens the album, and begins to leaf through it with a look of fond recollection.

I've always been one to take photos. Ever since I was a little kid and used to take pictures with my dad's Brownie. He called it a "box camera." It was just that—a black box with a fixed lens and this thin little toggle you shoved to one side to take a photograph. No f-stops or wide angles or telephotos or any of that. It was just a basic box. Come to think of it, everything was a basic box in those days: our house, our car . . . even most of my aunts. Things back then were built for endurance.

I keep my subjects in separate albums. An album for family, one for friends, one for vacations, and this one here for shots of my boyfriends. Or lovers, relationships . . . whatever. I get a real charge out of going through it every now and then, reflecting, putting myself back into those situations. Looking through it is like looking at the passing parade of the men in my life. *(She flips a page and reacts with laughter.)*

Oh Jesus! My God! Look at this shot of Harold and me taken up at Indian Lake. I must have been all of ninety pounds. And those legs. Like a couple of toothpicks stuck in a potato. This was taken when I was still in high school. Harold was my first. You know, the first I went all the way with. Or, thinking back on it, maybe we only went eighty percent. Harold was very handsome but awfully short, and I had to bend down to kiss him. He had trouble buying clothes and had to shop in the kids' department of Wren's department store. But he was very athletic and had a deep voice and was exceptionally strong. He could crunch a beer can with one hand back when they were made of steel. Harold was killed in Vietnam. *(She flips pages.)*

Oh! Here's Danny, Danny Mecklenberg. His father was a doctor and a big deal in town and Danny got to drive his Buick. It was as long as this room, with a bench seat, and had a physician's decal on the window, which was neat because we got to park illegally when we went to the movies. I went with Danny for almost a year. Until he went off to college. I think the thing I missed most about him was the Buick. (*She flips several pages.*)

Here's James, my first husband. James Addison Clark III. The biggest and bestest catch in the county. His father owned Clark Brass Foundry, and they lived near the country club in this huge Tudor house that looked like something out of Camelot. They, his family that is, they put on this front of liberalism, but they were really uppity, reactionary snobs. James had it all going for him—everything. That was his problem. He never had to scrap, you know. He just couldn't cope with the day-to-day of things—a job, a wife. He drank like crazy and went from this handsome, charming, athletic guy to a bloated wastrel. Maybe I wasn't patient enough. Maybe I should have hung in. Hell . . . who knows? Jim's still back in Springdale—a career drinker. (*She flips through the album.*)

Boy, is this ever a real rogues gallery, or what?

Ah. And here's Harold Simpson. Good old Harold square-ass Simpson. The good guy with the big smile and the wardrobe devoid of natural fiber. Just get a load of this outfit: a plaid jacket with a striped shirt and a paisley tie. Christ, he looks like network trouble.

Harold Simpson, the blue Banlon dream—the nicest guy ever born. Ingenuous right down to his acrylic socks. The guy didn't possess a grain of pretension. Everything about him was real except his clothes, which were right out of Dupont. I remember one time I bought him a box of Brooks Brothers shirts—one-hundred-percent cotton—and he said he couldn't wear them because they irritated his skin. He used them to polish his Pinto. Harold was a woodworker who fashioned the most beautiful furniture I've ever seen. And each piece reflected his love of making it. I used to watch him work. His hands moved over the wood as if it were human, caressing it with a loving care that transmitted itself into the very soul of the piece. And he never hurried. For Harold's work, time was an ally. Such a sweet guy. Damn . . . and I let 'im get away because he wasn't sophisticated. I was a stupid lady with screwed-up values who went for the veneer. Here was a real man and I wasn't mature enough to see it.

It's no wonder all I've got now is an old book full of faded photographs.

The used to photograph Shirley Temple through gause.
They should photograph me through linoleum.

Tallulah Bankhead (1902-1968)

Hanna, Back Then

HANNA

*Hanna, a woman with a clean country aspect, enters and
stands mid-stage. She looks off for a few seconds, drilling deep
into the past, into the great reservoir of her feelings for bygone
times. Through her lyrical ruminations, we learn how her in-
ability to accept the loss of her child destroyed her marriage,
irrevocably altered her life.*

How well I remember us
And how we were, back then,
Back in Nebraska, where the snows were long and
The winters seemed to never end.
Oh how young I was, back then.
And how young you were, my darling,
With your boyish ways and cowlicked hair
Thick as the alfalfa in the fields.
I can see me, I can see you, I can see us —
Back then a million Nebraska years ago.
It was good, back then,
When we were happy and in love with
An innocence only youth can know.
Then came your new job and the
Excitement of moving away
To a new place, a new city, a new life, a new house
With lots of rooms for our dreams to grow.
My, weren't you something?
With that new car
With that new job
With that big territory.
Weren't we special —
Weren't we something special to behold?
And then, for a sunshine hour, little Harry
Filled our life with joy, that darling little boy
Who was born without a chance,
Who grew so thin, so terribly, pitifully thin

That a stiff wind could pierce him if it tried.
Little Harry, just like a reed he was,
Just like a fragile little reed, nothing more;
But the little fellow never complained, never,
As he grew paler every day,
As he faded like chalk in the rain,
Fading, fading away.

After Harry, there was nothing for me,
But you, you had your job
And your new car
And that big territory
That seemed to gobble you up after Harry died.
Cleveland, Youngstown, Pittsburgh—Erie
Always Erie, it seemed.
You were never home. Never alone at home like me
With Harry alive on every wall, in every room,
His little voice a whisper never stilled.
You never knew what I went through—
It was as though someone had tipped me over
And poured me out till I was gone; and you,
You were always down in Erie, it seemed,
Always on the road in your new car
In your big territory.

So I had to ask, I had to know
About the attraction that kept you on the go.
She was a college girl, you said
Who went with you on long drives,
Even down to Wheeling once,
Who loved to ride with the windows down
Even in cold weather, while
She recited things from famous poets, and the like.
You said her voice was clear and soothing,
Blending with the sound of the engine of your car
As she rode with you,

Even down to Wheeling once.

We died with Harry, you said
As you packed your suitcase with the tarnished hasps
And laid in shirts and ties and other items neatly;
You said I'd changed completely:
Since the little lad had gone, I was a ghost
Of what I was before—back then.
Then, off you drove in your new car
Into your big territory, toward Erie and the
Poetess whose idyll's voice was soothing to your ear,
Leaving me standing with regret
For not being able to forget little Harry,
The wistful slip who never did complain
While he faded like crepe paper in the rain.
I wish for all the world it could be
Like it was before, back then,
So long ago, back then. (*She addresses a ghost OFF.*)
Harry . . . is that you?

See what the boys in the back room will have
And tell them I'm having the same.
See what the boys in the back room will have
And give me the poison they name.
And if I die, don't bring me a preacher
To witness all my follies and my shame;
Just see what the boys in the back room will have
And tell them I sighed—
And tell them I cried—
And tell them I died of the same!

Marlene Dietrich in *Destry Rides Again,* 1939

Harriet, Riches

HARRIET

Harriet, a trash picker/street person, wheels her junk-laden grocery cart to mid-stage.

Humble, my life is, you can call it humble. I'm a humble person living on the fruits of discarded America; a scavenger on the wastefulness of mankind, thanks to the great American passion—consuming. Buy it here, buy it there, buy it often and then—out the old window. You wouldn't believe the things that are discarded by the folks of this great city. Why, a person could start a department store called Elegant Trash and make a million easy. Yes sir, could make a mint. Half the stuff I pick up is in like-new condition, hardly used, never abused, not a scratch on it. You could give it for Christmas without hesitation. (*She pulls a toaster from her cart.*)

Like this here toaster. Now, just look at that, will you—more chrome than a '53 Buick. And just like new. Why, I'll bet this baby never browned even one slice of bread in its short, never-used life. And it's a Sunbeam, too—the best. As overadvertised and overpriced and oversold and overbought by people who probably hated toast in the first place. How the hell do ya figure? (*She replaces the toaster and withdraws a blouse.*)

Like this designer blouse—pure silk and hardly worn. Not even a trace of a perspiration ring. If it had, I wouldn't bother with it. I only pick up the best and the cleanest. A first-class salvager, that's me. Not like some of the others working the alleys and byways of this fair metropolis. Why, for this here one-hundred-percent Chinese silk blouse with a Liz Claiborne label, they've got to get a fortune. And here I go and pick it up for nothing because some spoiled beauty over on the west side couldn't be seen in the same thing twice. Now, is this a chuckle, or what? Why, people see you with the same skin, the same teeth, the same hands, the same frown, the same smile day after day, don't they? Like take this outfit I'm wearing, for instance. I'm going wear it till it feels pain and cries for mercy. Then I'll have it cleaned and burned. I work on a strictly no-frills basis. (*She replaces the blouse and grabs up a set of beautifully bound books.*)

Look here. Here's another discard of the overfed, under-read, TV-brained general public whose mind is on horizontal hold and who can't smile without a laugh track. What I've got in my hands right here are virgin tomes—unfingered volumes containing some of the best of Western Man's minds. Contained herein are great thoughts, high ideals, profound metaphors, and pithy aphorisms that have never been—and never will be—absorbed by the sit-com set. What a damned crying shame. Just look at this: Shakespeare, Dryden, Pope—one helluva lineup, a passel of profundity. Books bought for show, for decoration, to wallpaper some high-tech den in a million-dollar lean-to. And I get 'em for zip! The Bard for beans, Dryden for dirt, Pope for peanuts. (*She slams the books back into the cart and withdraws a calculator.*)

And here in my hand, ladies and gents, is one of the little marvels of the electronic age, one of the "things" that makes life soooo damn easy for today's lazy thinker . . . the calculator—the very latest in pocket technology that eliminates the need for us to learn how to add and subtract, divide, and do basic arithmetic. Why, any self-respecting grade-school student wouldn't be without one, no siree. Why learn your tables and memorize rules when you got it all right here in this little solar-operated baby? Why, it's got it all: it's got memory, it'll do addition, subtraction, multiplication, division, mixed calculation, constant calculation, power calculation, percentage calculation, add-on-discount calculation, memory calculation, square root, and more. All at the touch of an uneducated little finger. It's all in here thanks to tiny chips. Bless those little chips. (*Noting the price tag.*) And look, the price tag's still on it! No doubt never used because the owner wasn't capable of reading the instructions. So, onto the ever-growing mountain of trashed consumer goods it goes.

One heck of a poor damned profession for a woman, a degrading occupation, you're thinking, right? C'mon, sure you are—admit it. "Look at her," you say, "a woman disgracing herself by trudging up and down alleyways poking through the residue of human rot. Hasn't she any pride?" Well, folks, you're wrong, all wrong. I'm a dignified business woman who's doing a necessary job. I'm ridding the city of its guilt. I'm a guilt remover, you might say. The stuff I remove is no longer a reminder to people of their wasteful ways, no longer a back-alley testimonial to their disgraceful habit of overspending and overloading and acquiring that which is superfluous. The old guilt remover from the far-away hills, that's me. Harriet Blackfield, a twice-married, twice-divorced, well-educated trash picker; a free spirit, philosopher, and all-'round grubby street person who relieves society of its disgrace. I pay no taxes, sleep where I fall, and have a well-balanced diet from the gourmet trash cans of the well-heeled. It's great to be living in the USA. (*She snatches the toaster from the cart and extends it invitingly.*) Wanna buy a toaster? Cheap?

*For the theatre one needs long arms; it is better
to have them too long than too short. An artiste
with short arms can never, never make a fine gesture.*

Sarah Bernhardt (Sarah Henriette Rosine Bernard, 1844-1923)

Mary, Letting Go

MARY

Mary enters carrying variously colored, helium-inflated balloons suspended from strings.

I used to be earthbound and terribly restricted and narrow because I was constricted by fear; fear of people and new situations—the fear of letting go. And I was afraid of anything that involved real feelings. I was so damned uptight, so predictably safe. My life was colorless, empty, regimented, and boring as hell. There was a thick layer of dust on my soul. And love . . . I didn't have the slightest sense of it. And I needed it, like everybody needs it, must have it if they ever expect to blossom and grow. But I wouldn't let it in because I was so damned afraid of being hurt, of being used, taken advantage of. So, I shut people out. I shut life out. I was this living fossil going through the motions of being a person. I squelched opportunities for involvement time and time again until, after awhile . . . after awhile, there were no opportunities left because people became damned sick and tired of running headlong into the Great Wall of Mary. So slowly, little by little, over time, my potentials for intimacy disintegrated, and I became this insulated, isolated person. I'd resigned myself to loneliness—and it was hell.

Some nights my loneliness would attack me, and I could feel it deep in me, gnawing away at me like this big emotional cancer. Like most pain, it's difficult to describe. You can't. But if you've ever visited the cellar of loneliness, if you've ever been down there, you know the kind of pain I mean.

For a while, I made a stupid attempt to get involved by hanging out in singles bars which resulted in me meeting this guy, Stephen. I know it was a stupid thing to do, but at a certain point you fall victim to your desperation. The thing was doomed from the start, I knew that, but I plunged and we had this affair, which was totally dishonest because we were both looking for a quick fix, an emotional Band-Aid. Sex between us was purely a release—there was no love in it. After awhile, I became lonely *with* Steve; a loneliness that was just an unbearable solitude. So I cut it off, I got out. The whole thing was a stopgap, degrading experience that ended on a sour note and set me back to the point where I withdrew into myself completely. I became a fucking emotional hermit. Then, one day on lunch break, I decided to have my sandwich in the park. It was a bright, sunny, spring day. One of those kind of days that seemed brand new, like it'd just been unwrapped, you know. And in the park there was this balloon vendor who was inflating balloons with helium and tying them with strings and attaching them to his cart. The balloons floated above the cart like this big, buoyant, colorful bouquet. It was really neat. Then, one of the balloons, a bright yellow one, broke free and began to float upwards against the blue sky. (*She releases a yellow balloon and it soars upward, out of sight, into the flies.*)

I watched it as it fishtailed upwards and I thought, wow!, this balloon is like declaring its independence from the earth. It was a simple thing, I know, but profound. Here was this balloon breaking free from the pack and soaring off just as big as you please, thumbing its pretty yellow nose at its earthbound brothers stuck down there on the cart. I thought, Hey, why can't people do that? Why can't *I*? Then suddenly, it was clear. All I had to do was let go, break free, take charge of my life. I guess all the therapy and the conversations and all of the soul-searching and private agony needed some crazy little thing like this to make it all fall into place. And this was it, when I turned the corner, when I decided once and for all to get rid of the baggage. So . . . I let go of the guilt. (*She releases another balloon.*) I let go of my neurotic need to be my own prisoner. (*She releases another balloon.*) I let go of my fear of showing my feelings. (*She releases another balloon.*) I just let it *all go*. (*She releases all the balloons.*)

Doris, Expectations

DORIS

A telephone on a stand, next to a chair, is ringing with impatient persistence. Doris, towel-drying her hair, clad in a robe, enters.

It never fails. Never. Like every time I wash my hair, take a shower, or go to the bathroom, the fucking telephone rings. I'll never be a lonely person; I never have to worry about that. If I ever get lonely, I'll just go to the john. Who the hell, anyway, at this time of night. Jerks! (*She snatches up the receiver impatiently.*) Look, do you realize that it's, it's . . . (*She quickly drops her harshness and adopts a pleasant, conciliatory tone.*) Oh! it's you. No no, no problem. I was just sitting here watching the tube. Sure I remember you, don't tell me. You're the guy with the . . . the beard and red Reeboks. Oh yeah, sure, that's right—red hair and penny loafers. Roger, right? Oh yeah, Fred. Sure, Fred—right. I sometimes, like, get things a little mixed up, ya know? To be honest, remembering isn't my long suit. I'm like what you might call your abstract thinker. Friday? Yeah, I guess so, sure. Yeah, why not? A play? Hey, that sounds neat. Okay, see you at seven Friday. 134 Maple, Apartment B. Right. (*She hangs up.*) I hope he's the cute one. One was kind of dorky and gangly like he was made out of sucker sticks. No, the red-haired guy was the cutie. Whatta doll. And he's taking me to a play. Hey, *that's* different. (BLACKOUT.)

(*LIGHTS UP. Doris ENTERS wearing a raincoat, a dreamy expression. She sighs.*) He was a dream. I can't believe it. Most of the guys you meet are one-hundred-percent nerds. But Freddy . . . he's beautiful. And intellectual. He knows all about plays and art and books even. There's no end to this guy's mental. If it wasn't for him, I wouldn't have understood beans about the play. My impression was that it was about this nose-picker and this whore who loved to smack the crap out of each other because they hated nuclear power. Fred said it was something-gorical. Sharp. A mind like a Bic razor, this guy. Then, after the show, he took me to this neat little Italian place, where he ordered in honest-to-goodness Italian. Here I am, sitting here listening to a regular Marcello Mastroianni. Most of the fucking airheads I date do this broken Italian routine by adding an "a" to everything. "We'll have-a nice-a bottle-a wine-a." Drips! (*She hums a few bars of "That's Amore." The phone rings, she answers.*) Yes? Oh, Fred, hi! Yes, I had a *won*derful time. It was one of the best nights I can remember. You, too? That's nice. And the play was terrific, after you explained it, that is, and I understood about it being paragorical. You do? Well, I think you're sweet, too. Honest? Really? You mean it? That's nice, Freddy. Sure, I'd love to. Tomorrow night? Sure, great. See you at seven. Bye. (*She replaces the receiver.*) This may be rushing it, but what the hell? When it's right, it's right, ya know. When the bell rings, answer it. You sit back and act cool, you wind up freezing to death. (*Sings.*) "Fools rush in, where wise men fear to tread. . . ." A woman's lucky if she meets a man like Freddy once in her lifetime. Most of the men you meet are oversexed macho slobs who haven't got a brain to their fucking name. You look in their eyes and you see the backs of their heads. This time, Doris, you're onto a winner, a class act. And not even once did he pull any goofy baloney; he didn't tell me once I had nice eyes or a great bod or any of that slider crap, or stare at me like I was the window at Frederick's of Hollywood. He's a very high-minded person with a high IQ and high moral standards. It sticks out all over him so far you could hang something on it. And he's gorgeous. (*She walks OFF humming, "That's Amore." BLACKOUT.*)

(*LIGHTS UP. Doris ENTERS wearing her robe, carrying a mug of coffee. We can hear the shower running OFF. A pair of trousers are conspicuous over the chair.*) This can't be earth. It's heaven! I'm pinching myself so much I look like I'm tattooed. Life is wonderful. When you're in love, it's just not a piece of cake, it's a chocolate factory with whipped cream and nuts and a maraschino cherry the size of a weather balloon.

Ecstasy, the poets call it. I call it, wowee! Just four weeks now and already I'm a new person; so happy and full of joy my heart feels like blowing right through my chest—excuse the expression. Freddy's like nobody I've ever known. He's kind and considerate and understanding and gentle. That's the thing that impresses me most of all, his gentleness, you know. And he loves *me,* Doris Bernstein from the wrong part of Shaker Heights—the part with all the Polish funeral homes. This should happen to me? And he's got something important to say to me today, something *special!* I'm so excited. I'd call my mother, but I don't need advice. (*LIGHTS SLOWLY TO BLACK.*)

(*LIGHTS UP. Doris is sitting dejectedly in the chair. She appears a mess, hair askew. The phone rings. And rings. Finally, she answers weakly.*) Hello. (*Her voice goes full strength.*) What? Are you kidding? you sonofabitch! You bastard. You asshole! You've got a lot of nerve calling up here! Haven't you got any pride? I don't care. It's over! You hurt me, Freddy. You gave me hope and built me up and then it all came down to a lie. You can do a lot of things to a woman, Freddy, but you don't use them, because that's the one thing they'll never forgive you for. It's over, understand, over! Go shit on somebody else's heart! (*She slams the receiver.*) And for once I thought I was onto something special. For the first time, I thought heaven had moved into this little second-floor mess and from now on life was gonna be a great big plate of knishes. Then the sonofabitch tells me he's a married man. I shoulda known. He was too perfect. Nobody who looks like chrome can be unattached. So, here I am, back into being out of love. Back to insomnia and scorched coffee. Back to dating drips who can't find it with both hands. Sometimes I think unhappiness is like this shadow—you just can't shake it no matter how hard you try. Damn. Is there ever a picnic without ants? (*The phone begins to ring again. She allows it to ring, looking at it forlornly. Then she stands and walks off into the darkness as the phone continues to bleat.*)

I wish I had invented sex. Sex is number one.

Brigitte Bardot (1933–   )

Lee Ann, Home Cookin'

LEE ANN

LIGHTS UP on Lee Ann, who is standing behind a table mid-stage. On the table are a Dutch oven, a large bowl, a can of pepper, and a container full of water. If budget permits, and realism is your aim, the actual ingredients may be utilized—a two-pound cottage ham, two pounds of green beans, ten small red potatoes—or you may pantomime. In either case, however, a Dutch oven, bowl, pepper, and water are necessary.

Well sir, ladies, it's sure a real pleasure t' be invited t' yer little gormett cookin' school. Not too often a countrified person like me gits t' rub shoulders with the likes o' folks who went past the eighth grade. Down 'round where I come from, Jenkins, Kentucky, most people my age had t' git out and buckle down t' business when they was just kiddies. Why, my mom an' daddy hardly had any edjacation atall. But they was work-willin', God-fearin' folks alivin' in the shadow o' the cross. An' my momma had t' learn how t' whip up a meal in short or-der 'fore she went t' the first grade. An' lemme tell ya, ladies, some a the stuff that rolled outta that there little kitchen o' hers was s' dern lip-smackin' delicious they oughta had passed a law agin it. It was rich an' flavorful an' down-home plain, not fancy-mincy. You go an' set somethin' fancy-mincy in front a the fellas in my county—them boys who git up 'fore breakfast and do the work o' three men an' a boy—an' yer gonna have hades on yer hands, lemme tell ya.

Now, I know all about yer fancy cookin'. I seen pitchers of it an' recipes fer it in yer fancy Frenchy magazines, ~~an' I've watched yer Julia Child and some o' them other high-powered cooks on the TV.~~ Well, sir, I ain't much impressed. ~~Here ya have swimmin' 'round in a lake o' runny glop a little bitty~~ hunk o' meat, three peas and a carrot, an' a ~~piece~~ o' potata 'bout the size of a ~~quarter. One heckuva~~ lookin' sight. Between you an' me, ~~it looks like somethin' at~~ the bottom of a ~~birdcage.~~ Why, that ain't eatin', that there's ~~messin' 'round~~

with playhouse food. Ain't no way anyone's gonna walk away from the table satisfied after eatin' a meal you can put on a Ritz cracker. No way, sister. An' they charge a fortune fer that cute crap, too. Highway robbery. My cousin Ralph—a big man with the government up in Cleveland—said he paid over a hunnert dollars fer dinner one time. Can you imagine? With people agoin' hungry! No wonder the country's goin' t' hades in a handcart. When people ask me what gormett is, I tell 'im gormett's anythin' that tastes *wonderful*: a cheeseburg, a chili-dog, rice an' beans—anythin' that makes yer mouth sit up an' water, anythin' that satisfies an' gratifies an' makes yer stom-ach an' yer mouth best friends. Only one kind o' food, an' that's food that's plain, fresh, plentiful, well-cooked, an' well-seasoned.

Well, now, ya asked me t' bring 'long a real country recipe, so a did. What I'm gonna show ya how t' throw together here is a mess o' ham an' beans an' potatas. 'Bout as good as it gits, ladies, 'bout as good as it gits. First off, ya go out an' git yer-self a two-pound cottage ham, like this' un here. (*She holds up the ham proudly.*) Now, whatever ya do, don't go fer yer fancy cut a meat, no sir. Buy yerself a cheaper piece that's loaded with fat. Remember, this ain't no health food we're talkin' 'bout here, ladies, we're talkin' 'bout good eatin', stuff ya don't have t' hide with a bunch o' cream sauce, a bunch a runny gook that's got more fat in it than this here entire ham. Okay. Now, ya put yer ham inta yer Dutch oven. Slap it right on in there. (*She places the ham in the Dutch over and gives it a few friendly pats.*) Now. (*She displays a bowlful of green beans.*) Ya take about two pound o' green beans that have been warshed in cold water, an' ya add 'em in with yer ham. (*Under her monologue, she snaps the beans and adds them to the Dutch oven.*) I brought these here beans up with me from Jenkins. Picked 'em right out a m' garden 'fore I left. You ain't gonna find no beans like these here in no supermarket, but, what the heck, ya can't have everthing. Just listen t' these little rascals snap in two, will ya. Sounds just like I'm breakin' bones up here. 'Nother thing—these here beans ain't never been sprayed with no pesticides. Stuff they dump on food nowadays, why heck, ya don't know what it's gonna do to ya. All kinds a chemicals an' junk in the food we eat anymore. Scary. Someday, everone in America's gonna light up jus' like a chest X-ray. Chemicals—ya can't trust 'em. (*She tosses in the last of the beans and takes up the pitcher of water.*) All right, now. Now ya add 'bout six cups o' water. (*She pours the water into the Dutch oven.*) There we go! Okay, now we shake in a little bit o' pepper. (*She peppers the concoction liberally.*)My grandaddy, rest 'is soul, my grandaddy used t' say pepper was no good 'cause it's half p's—**p**-e-**p**-**p**-e-r. Git it? Okay, now what ya wanna do is slam a cover on this baby an' pop it inta yer oven an' cook it on a low heat so's it's barely a simmerin'—fer two hours. Then, then ya take it out an' add in ten or so little red potatas, like I got me here. (*She displays the potatoes in the bowl*.) Ain't them cute? You add them t' the ham an' beans and let it all cook real slow fer 'bout another hour. And that's it. Simple. Nothin' to it. And then ya serve it up with a batch o' hot cornbread an' butter. No margarine—*real* butter.

Well, ladies, there ya have it. Ole-fashioned ham an' beans an' potatas. Sweet eatin'. The best.

Put me in the last fifteen minutes of a picture and I don't care what happened before. I don't even care if I was in the rest of the damned thing—I'll take it in those fifteen minutes.

Barbara Stanwyck (Ruby Stevens, 1907-1990)

Sally, Sweat

SALLY

DISCO MUSIC UP. Sally, a real dynamo both physically and verbally, jogs briskly on stage clad in lycra-spandex aerobic togs, sneakers—the whole complement of hip work-out attire. She is a bundle of energy and is an incessant talker. She does a series of jumping and stretching movements to a relentless rock rhythm. Then, MUSIC DOWN AND UNDER to a point that will enable us to hear her monologue. She moves about frequently during her speech, stretching, jumping, running in place.

I've been heavy into aerobics for about two years now. My neighbor, Sherrie—a really hot lady who's into everything—convinced me I should get off my saggy buns and get moving. Sherrie is an aerobics freak. She can turn herself into a rubber band. And she's as hard as a rock. You should see her glutes and quads and lats. She makes Jane Fonda look like a bowl of warm Jello. Before I started working out, I was this really lethargic overeater who wouldn't move for anything. I was to the point where if I'd forget to take the remote control to my chair, I'd watch whatever was on the tube rather than get up to change channels. One night I sat through a Broderick Crawford film festival. Also, my body was in sad shape. My skin was like hanging moss. The backs of my legs looked like pearl tapioca. I didn't dare go near the beach anymore because I was afraid someone would harpoon me. My best friends were *any* kind of junk food: Twinkies, Goobers, Big Macs, pizza, ice cream, jellybeans—you name it. If it was soft and you didn't have to cook it, I glommed it up. I was floating in palm oil and coconut oil. I had more sodium in me than the Dead Sea. I was this great human garbage disposal. I wore nothing but loose-fitting clothing—things I could wear hanging out; oversized stuff that covered up the festoons of undulating flab underneath. I weighed a ton. The seat of my Mustang had to be resprung twice. And at night, in bed, my boyfriend, Jerry, kept rolling over into me all the time. I was a fast-expanding, fast-food junkie who looked like her favorite appliance—a refrigerator. I kept kidding myself, promising myself and Jerry I'd go on a diet. And I would. Until I'd get this overpowering Raisinette urge. For the first week, I'd loose a bunch of weight fast—water loss of tidal-wave proportions. Then I'd hit a sticking point, and nothing! So, what the hell. Back to the calories. I was up and down in weight so much it's a wonder my stomach doesn't look like a concertina. It was living a nightmare. Then it all came crashing down on me one night when I got into an argument with Jerry and he called me Burger Butt. That hurt. Sticks and stones can only break my bones, but being called names hurts. Burger Butt, Munchie Mouth—he hit me with some damned awful names, the worst being Fat Ass! That really got me thoroughly pissed. But, you know . . . he was right and I knew it and I knew I had to do something about my weight before I exploded and blew up all over the house. Pity the poor guys who would have had the job of scraping the pieces off the walls. They would've died of sugar diabetes.

That's when I met Sherrie. I was waddling along Elm Street one day, devouring a pound of lard on a stick, or something, when along she comes running along like deer in heat, showing virtually no signs of fatigue. I was kinda acquainted with her because she lived on the next block and I used to see her every now and then when I was at the supermarket buying up sides of beef or jumbo packs of anything without roughage. Apparently she could tell I was depressed because she stopped and we started talking, and I told her how great and lean she looked and how it made me sick because I ate more than she weighed for breakfast. She was very sincere and sympathetic and understanding and honestly seemed to care. (*She ceases moving and her mood shifts to one of seriousness for a few seconds. MUSIC OUT.*) Most people don't. To most of them, what you are is an embarrassment and they stay away from you because they don't want to be seen in your company. Being fat is not fun, even though I'm kidding about it now. It's a devastating thing—a social crippler. You try to laugh it off, go along with all of the jokes, but underneath, you're hurting, dying. Obeseness attacks the mind as well as the body and effects you in profoundly negative ways. Before I made a serious commitment to change, I was like this really terribly unhappy, fearful person. . . . But, anyway . . . back to Sherrie. . . . (*MUSIC UP. She resumes movement, once more in a buoyant mood.*) Sherrie convinced me that I should come with her to her health club. I met her there the next morning. We tried to find an outfit that would fit me, but no luck. So I wound up taking my first aerobics lessons in a raincoat.

At first, I didn't think I'd make it. It was sheer torture: nonstop movement and stretching and trying to stick your shoe in your ear. For the first few weeks, I couldn't sleep because I couldn't find a spot to lie on that wasn't sore. It was a killer. But I hung in, and little by little I began to loosen up and my weight started to drop because of this rabbit-food diet Sherrie had me on. The rule was: if it tasted good—*don't eat it*! I went from burger breath to broccoli breath and eventually from fat ass to tight tush. The weight started to peel away and alluva sudden I discovered that there was somebody else under all the sausage. And the classes became easier and my endurance improved and I kept stepping up the difficulty of my aerobics program. Until now—I'm an instructor at the club on Wednesdays and Fridays. My life has turned around completely and I feel great and Jerry is into weight training and we play tennis and run and we both have bikes. Last Sunday we rode forty miles, jogged for three, and then came home and worked out on the Stair Master. And when we went to bed, Jerry didn't roll to my side once. At least, not accidentally.

The most important thing a woman can have,
next to her talent, of course, is her hairdresser.

Joan Crawford, (1906-1977)

Dolly, Motel 6

DOLLY

Dolly is sitting at the edge of a rumpled bed. She is wearing panties and a bra. The rest of her clothing is draped over a nearby chair.

He was wonderful. Nice and big. I like 'em big. One thing I don't like for sure is a little bitty puny man. Nothing much to get hold of, if you know what I mean. Scrawny men make me sick. I've always liked big men since I was old enough to know better. My daddy was a big man. Over six feet tall.

(*Noting the bed.*) Just look at this bed, will ya. A person can tell what went on just by lookin' at it. So, well . . . I reckon this here mess tells ya that there was a whole lotta shakin' goin' on. (*Pause.*) You can bet on one thing, he won't forget about Dolly for a while, no way. When I get hold of 'em, I turn 'em every which way and then turn 'em again. This one was different, though, not like a lot of other guys. He was gentle. Some guys are real rough when they do it, like they're gettin' even for something. (*She rises and goes to the window and peers out.*)

Another rainy day. Seems like the winters go on forever in this here jerk-off town. One of these days I'm gonna quit my job at the mill and move to a big city. Maybe up to Pittsburgh, where they don't roll the whole thing up like a damp shirt when the sun goes down. I met this real nice guy up there, too. He was in real estate. Said he got into real estate 'cause his daddy told him to get a lot while he was young. I like men with a sense of humor. (*She goes to the chair and begins to dress.*)

My husband, Dwayne, he don't see any humor in anything. He can sit through the Flintstones reruns and never crack a smile once. What a dud. If Barney Rubble can't get to ya, what the hell can? He just sits there in his Barca-lounger and drinks Bud and burps. He hasn't made it with me in over six months. He should just go and cut that little thing of his off for all the good it does 'im. I think he whacks off, though. I'm sure of it. He spends way too much time in the bathroom. I read this article, in the *Woman's Day*, ya know, about how lots of men whack off and think of other women while they're doin' it. I wonder who Dwayne thinks of. He isn't thinkin' of me, that's for sure.

This guy, the one I met this morning over to the bowling alley coffee shop? He was a salesman for Xerox. He was real cute and wore a suit and tie and he smelled real nice. Most of the men around here don't dress for shit. They run around in ripped Levis and stupid baseball caps. No-class shitkickers with big beer tumors under their shirts. Their whole life, day after day, is working, stopping off at the Dixie Tavern, and then coming home half-pissed and falling asleep in front of the TV.

Guys who come through town, salesmen and the like, usually stop off at the bowling alley 'cause they serve good coffee. They put chicory in it. I've met some real nice fellas over there. This one guy was this musician on his way to New York. He was real cute. We spent the whole afternoon over here at the Motel 6, and we went through an entire bottle of Southern Comfort. Comfort's my favorite. Although you gotta be careful about guys drinkin' too much 'cause sometimes they can't get it up. Alcohol affects some men that way. Nothing worse than trying to get it on with wilted lettuce. (*She combs her hair with an off-handed, casual air.*) And these day you gotta use all kinds of protection, too.

When Dwayne and I were first married, we used to get it on all the time. Of course, we'd done it way before that. We started when we were in high school. Dwayne was a shop major. He cut off the tip of his little finger with a bench saw. May's well cut off his pecker, too, like I said. For the first couple of years of our marriage, we got along good. Then I lost our baby and he blamed me for it. Like it was my fault, you know. Anyway, that changed things between us, and good old Dwayne turned from poppin' me t' poppin' the tops off Buds and watchin' TV. He watches mostly cops shows with all that macho gun bullshit. I hate guns.

I'm too romantic a person to give up sex at my age. So, I have these little romances here at the motel. They have cable television, and this room has a vibrator bed. For a quarter you get cheap thrills. Not a bad place, but they're always outta ice. (*She applies lipstick heavily.*) To me, love-makin's a beautiful experience, ya know. Besides, a person should never have any bad feelings about sex because it's just a natural thing. When a woman spreads her legs, it's like she's openin' up her soul, in a way. It's like she's saying, "Here I am, wide open and beautiful, all of me, every bit of me, free and wonderful." Lots of women don't understand. A lot of 'em do it because it's like this duty, like this job, or because they think they owe it to some dude because he buys 'em a burger an' fries. I know it for a fact. I talk to these women all the time when I'm gettin' my hair dyed over at Rosie Whitfield's shop. Most of 'em haven't got a clue about how to enjoy that beautiful flower right there between their legs. For them it's either a weapon or a reward.

You can bet your sweet business there's plenty of talk about me going on in this one-horse place. But do you think I give a damn? Hell no. They can say whatever they want. Besides, it gives 'em something to do. Most of their lives are rusted-out and up on blocks. Come to think if it, when it comes to livin', I've got a feeling that most people are just like Dwayne—in the bathroom, whackin' off!

ORDER DIRECT